THE
UNICORN'S SECRET

#6

True Heart

by Kathleen Duey
illustrated by Omar Rayyan

ALADDIN PAPERBACKS

New York   London   Toronto   Sydney   Singapore

For all the daydreamers . . .

This book is a work of fiction. Any references to historical events, real people, or real locales are used fictitiously. Other names, characters, places, and incidents are the product of the author's imagination, and any resemblance to actual events or locales or persons, living or dead, is entirely coincidental.

First Aladdin Paperbacks edition April 2003

Text copyright © 2003 by Kathleen Duey
Illustrations copyright © 2003 by Omar Rayyan

ALADDIN PAPERBACKS
An imprint of Simon & Schuster
Children's Publishing Division
1230 Avenue of the Americas
New York, NY 10020

Also available in an Aladdin Library edition.
Designed by Debra Sfetsios
The text of this book was set in Golden Cockerel ITC.

Printed in the United States of America
2 4 6 8 10 9 7 5 3 1
ISBN 0-689-85370-X

The Library of Congress Control Number for the Library Edition is 2002113022

✦

Joseph Lequire has finished Moonsilver's armor. The silvery metal hides his horn. Heart is delighted—but she is worried, too. It has taken Tibbs and the metalsmith three days to make the armor. Where are the Gypsies? Have Lord Irmaedith's guards taken them to Bidenfast? Why? Are they safe?

✦

✦CHAPTER ONE

Heart stood in the stone doorway.

The early chill was sharp.

Her breath made clouds of soft mist.

Kip sat beside her, his furry shoulder warm against her leg.

Heart stared at the yellow-orange glow in the valley below. The river of fire looked even stranger in the dark.

Heart knew that the sun would rise soon.

When it did, she would have to leave.

"I wish you could stay," Tibbs said from behind her.

Heart turned.

Tibbs looked tired.

He and Joseph had worked hard to finish

Moonsilver's armor quickly.

"I don't want to leave," Heart admitted. She felt the silver bracelet tighten on her wrist for an instant.

As always, it startled her.

As always, she wasn't sure what it meant.

"But you have to go," Tibbs said.

Heart nodded. The forge felt safe, but it wasn't, not for her—and not for the unicorns. Too many nobles came here.

Heart bit her lip, wishing she could be sure where the unicorns *would* be safe.

Maybe her family would help one day.

Or maybe she would never find them.

For now, all she could do was find the Gypsies.

She thought about Binney and smiled. It would be so good to know they were all safe, to be back with her friends.

"Keep learning to read, keep practicing," Tibbs said softly.

Heart met his eyes. "I will."

Tibbs frowned. "My master in Derrytown was

nervous about teaching me. It's usually just for the nobility, you know."

Heart looked at him. "A woman in Yolen's Crossing offered to teach me."

"Was she dressed fancy?" Tibbs asked.

Heart nodded.

Tibbs was silent for a moment. He shrugged. "The lords all forbid books for common folk. Dunraven is the strictest, my master said."

Heart nodded. She had lived her whole life in Ash Grove and had never even known what a book *was*.

"Can Ruth Oakes read?" she asked Tibbs.

He shrugged again. "I don't know. She never said so."

"She never told me, either," Heart said. "But maybe she would keep it secret."

They were both silent for a long moment.

Heart looked back into the beautiful house. It would be wonderful to stay here, to practice reading with Tibbs, to stop traveling—to have a home.

"Thank Joseph for me," she said aloud.

Tibbs nodded. "I will."

"It's been three days," Heart said, looking up at Tibbs.

"You'll find the Gypsies," he answered, understanding her instantly. Then he pointed. "Look."

Heart faced the valley.

Avamir was grazing.

Moonsilver was prancing easily down the slope.

He reared, turning, then trotted upward again.

The armor shone orange yellow in the light from the fiery river.

The plumes swayed.

Heart laughed. Moonsilver was lifting his hooves high, like a horse in a parade. He was showing off.

He looked beautiful.

The armor fit perfectly.

It was as strong as real armor, but not as heavy.

Joseph had cut curved pieces out of the metal that covered Moonsilver's back and sides.

Joseph said horses sometimes died of heat sickness in closed armor, so Moonsilver's was made to be cooler too. The base of the thin silver spike that enclosed his horn had four narrow slits in it.

The top was open.

Only an eyelash-thick crescent of his horn tip showed, but air could pass through. There were slits in the cheek plates, too.

Tibbs was smiling. "He seems to like it."

Heart nodded and looked at the sky. It was almost time to leave.

They were ready.

Her carry-sack was full of bread, barley, and wrinkled autumn apples from Joseph's root cellar.

She had her flints. Joseph had given her half a candle.

He had given her soft cotton rope, too. She had braided halters for the unicorns while he and Tibbs worked on the armor.

Avamir and Moonsilver had allowed her to put them on.

"I should go with you," Tibbs said quietly.

Heart met his eyes. "No, you shouldn't. You have finally found your home."

Tibbs looked into her eyes for a long moment.

"Thank you, Heart. You are a true friend."

Heart took a deep breath. "I only hope I can find mine."

Tibbs reached out and touched her cheek. "You will. If you see Ruth Oakes, tell her how happy I am. Tell Binney I have doubled my skill already, just helping Joseph on the armor."

Tibbs's eyes were full of joy.

"I will tell them," Heart said.

"Try not to worry," Tibbs told her. "Binney and Zim probably talked the guardsmen around in circles and made friends of them by the time they got to Bidenfast."

Heart sighed. "Or maybe the new Lord Irmaedith heard rumors about a unicorn."

Tibbs frowned. "Maybe."

Heart scuffed at the ground. If the Gypsies were in trouble because of helping her . . .

She pulled in a deep breath. The sunrise was shading the sky gold pink along the horizon now. "Where is Joseph?"

"Snoring," Tibbs said. "He lay down to rest and

went out like a candle."

Heart smiled. "Thank him—for all of us."

"I will," Tibbs said. "Come back if you can."

"I'll try," Heart promised.

Avamir whinnied, high and clear.

Tibbs smiled. "M'Lady Unicorn summons you, I think."

Heart stepped out of the doorway into the chilly morning.

"Good-bye," Tibbs said.

Heart smiled at him, then started down the steep, rocky path.

+CHAPTER TWO

Heart could feel waves of heat rising from the river of melted rock.

It felt wonderful in the chill, like a hearth blaze.

Kip barked twice, then settled into a trot at her heels.

Halfway down, the unicorns broke into a gallop.

They leaped the fiery current.

Kip tore off after them, streaking toward the little bridge.

Heart put her carry-sack over her shoulder and began to run.

She ran as fast as she could.

It wasn't nearly fast enough.

At the bottom of the slope Moonsilver and Avamir waited for her.

Avamir tossed her head, jingling the tiny Gypsy bells Talia and Josepha had braided into her mane.

Kip ran in circles, barking.

Avamir stamped a forehoof, looking at him.

Kip quieted.

"I'd better go first," Heart told Avamir. "In case we meet anyone on the path."

Avamir shook her mane and lowered her head, waiting for Heart to start off.

The path was narrow and steep. Heart walked carefully until the sun rose.

Then, with the morning light pouring over the Earth, she hurried along, her carry-sack over her shoulder.

Kip raced ahead.

His paws were nearly soundless on the path.

The unicorns were almost as quiet.

Their hooves seemed barely to touch the earth.

As she walked, Heart's spirits rose. The rhythm of her own steps felt wonderful. The scent of the pine trees soothed her worries a little.

At the bottom of the path she stopped.

"Wait here," she told the unicorns. "It's important that no one sees us coming down from the forge."

Avamir tossed her head, but she didn't follow as Heart walked out through the trees.

Heart moved slowly and carefully, listening for voices.

She slowed, crossing the grassy place where the Gypsies had camped.

There was a bright-colored scarf in the grass.

Heart picked it up, fingering the silk.

The Gypsies had broken camp fast.

Too fast.

Heart had seen the guards shouting at them.

Feeling her worries rise, Heart tied the scarf around her neck.

She eased forward, then listened again before she stepped out of the trees.

The road was empty as far as she could see in both directions.

She turned and called out to Kip and the unicorns.

Kip barked and dashed forward. The unicorns

cantered gracefully through the dappled sunlight, then slowed once they got close.

Heart led off, walking fast.

The morning was cool and bright. The road dust had been settled by a heavy dew.

The birds were wide awake.

Their songs overlapped and blended, a tangled chorus.

Heart lengthened her stride.

She wanted to get as far from the forge path as she could before anyone saw them.

If the guardsmen had been looking for Moonsilver, she didn't want anyone to guess that Joseph had helped her.

She didn't want to bring him trouble.

Kip barked suddenly and raced off through the trees.

Heart watched him go and smiled. He loved chasing squirrels.

She glanced at Moonsilver.

Moonsilver looked like a lord's horse now, not a unicorn.

Avamir's braided halter made her look like a well-bred stable mare. A little thin, maybe, but beautiful.

"But I still look like a Gypsy girl," Heart said aloud. She flipped her sash and jingled the tiny bells tied into the fringe.

Avamir whuffled a long breath out through her nostrils.

"I do, though," Heart said, turning. "What will people think when they . . ."

The mare lifted her head sharply and turned to look back down the road.

Heart stopped midsentence and turned.

She saw the shape of someone walking toward them in the early light.

There were woods on either side of the road.

It didn't matter.

It was too late to hide.

Heart pulled the Gypsy scarf from her neck.

She put it in her carry-sack.

✦CHAPTER THREE

Avamir moved closer to Heart. Moonsilver came up on her other side.

Heart reached up carefully and took hold of their halters. Then she turned again.

The woman coming up behind them looked familiar. She was waving, gesturing for Heart to stop.

"Who are you?" the woman called out.

Her voice was sharp.

The forest became silent.

All the songbirds stopped singing.

The woman walked through a patch of sunlight, and Heart saw that she was carrying an armload of books.

Heart felt her stomach tighten. It was the woman

from Thoren who had been so rude to her and Tibbs when they'd asked to look at a book.

Kip growled low in his throat.

He glanced up at Heart.

"Shhh," Heart warned him.

"Who are you?" the woman demanded again. "I asked you a question! Are you a page?" She scowled. "Whose horses do you lead so boldly down the High Road?"

Heart wasn't sure what to say.

The woman would recognize her any second, she was sure.

"They are trusted to me," she finally managed.

It was true, in a way, but she knew the woman would never believe it.

Fine horses in armor belonged to lords—no one else could afford them.

The woman tilted her head to one side as she came closer, her eyes fierce. "And what lord are you serving? Is he here for the new Lord Irmaedith's crowning?"

Heart was silent.

She pretended to fuss with Avamir's halter.

"Are you on your way to Bidenfast?" the woman asked a little louder.

Heart nodded slowly.

She was.

That was where the guards had said they were taking the Gypsies.

Was that where the crowning was to be?

"Am I on the right road, ma'am?" Heart tried hard to sound very polite.

The woman clicked her tongue.

She circled the unicorns widely.

They all followed her with their eyes, turning as she came around to face them.

"You are. What lord do you serve?"

Heart took a deep breath. "We come from Dunraven's lands," she said, telling the truth in fact, if only in part.

"If Lord Dunraven has sent you to Bidenfast, he is going to the crowning," the woman said. Then she narrowed her eyes.

Heart held her breath.

"Why do you wear Gypsy clothes?" the woman

asked quietly. She leaned closer. "Answer! Have you *stolen* these horses?"

"No!" Heart said quickly. "I am the one who cares for them."

Moonsilver fidgeted.

Avamir tossed her head, nearly pulling Heart off her feet.

The motion made her sash swing, and the bells tinkled.

The woman's lips curled. "I remember you! You lied about learning to read."

"I didn't lie," Heart answered. "I am learning."

"If you are Lord Dunraven's page, prove it," the woman said coldly. She opened a book and thrust it at Heart.

Kip growled.

Heart touched his head and tried to calm him.

Avamir exhaled a fluttering breath.

Heart knew Avamir was too clever to make trouble now.

She knew that Moonsilver would stand quietly if his mother did.

She released the halters.

Then she reached out and took the book.

She held it carefully, her pulse thudding.

"Go on," the woman said. She tapped the page.

Heart stared at it.

The words were not simple.

"Read!" the woman snapped. "Or admit that you are lying."

Heart held the book with trembling hands.

"I haven't been able to practice enough," she said, looking up.

The woman laughed. "I was right. You are not nobility, high or low or any other kind. There are guards nearby, and I—"

"'C . . . Cas . . . Cas . . . Castle,'" Heart began desperately, interrupting. The woman stopped talking and glared at her.

"'Ava . . . Ava . . . mir,'" Heart managed. She frowned. "'Castle Avamir . . . ,'" she repeated, then stopped, startled at the words.

"Go on!" the woman commanded.

Heart tried to concentrate. It was hard. The woman was leaning close.

Heart took a deep breath.

"'Cas . . . Castle Avamir was long s . . . said to be in L . . . Lord Kay . . .Kaybale's f . . . for . . . forest,'" she read slowly, "'but th . . . this was not . . . t . . . t . . . true.'"

She looked up nervously.

The woman was staring at her, her mouth half open.

Heart looked back at the book. "'Castle Avamir was long said to be in Lord K . . . Kaybale's f . . . forest, but . . . this was not true,'" she repeated.

She joined the words much more smoothly the second time.

She took a deep breath. "'The tales of the cas . . . castle be . . . began when the uni . . . corns dis . . . dis . . . disappear . . . disappeared. The l . . . lords were—'"

"That's enough!" the woman interrupted.

Before Heart could react, she had snatched the book.

Heart reached out for it, desperate to read the rest.

"Manners!" the woman scolded. "Lord Dunraven may be teaching you to read, but you've learned little else!"

Heart forced herself to step back.

"Where *is* Castle Avamir?" she asked politely, trembling.

"Why should that concern you?" the woman asked sharply.

Heart pressed her lips together.

What could she possibly answer? That her name was Heart Avamir? That the design of the rearing unicorns had been embroidered in silver on her baby blanket? Heart clenched her fists—she had to say *something*. The woman was waiting, staring at her.

"I think my family might be from the Royal House of Avamir," Heart finally said in a low voice.

The woman inhaled sharply. "That is a dangerous joke."

Heart shook her head. "I didn't mean to—"

"Enough!" the woman said, cutting her off. "Go!

Begone! Take your stupid jests with you." She made a shooing motion with one hand. "The guards can sort you out," she mumbled. "I have books to be burned."

Kip growled again.

Avamir tossed her mane.

"Books to be *burned*?" Heart echoed, sure she had misheard. It made no sense. But the woman nodded vaguely. "Would you give me that book, then?" Heart said.

The woman laughed, a cracking, unhappy sound. She clutched the books close to her body.

"Give you a storybook? And risk someone finding out?" Without another word she walked away fast, veering onto a narrow path that Heart hadn't noticed.

She did not look back.

Heart stared after her.

Burned? That made no sense. The woman barely let anyone else touch her books. She must have said "returned."

Heart sighed. That meant some noble family

lived up that path. The woman was taking back books she had borrowed.

Heart shivered. It was still chilly.

Avamir nudged her.

Heart blinked. She was wasting time.

She began walking, but her fists were clenched.

Why should only noble families be allowed to read?

✦CHAPTER FOUR

That night, Heart and Kip curled up in a meadow not far from the road. Avamir and Moonsilver lay side by side a little way off. A thick stand of chestnut trees hid them all from anyone passing by on the road.

The next day, Heart woke early.

As they traveled, the road began to rise.

Binney had called this the High Road.

By noon Heart knew why. Her legs ached, and still the road steepened.

Late in the day Heart saw a farmer's cart ahead of them.

She slowed to match the pace of the clopping mules that pulled it.

She had to keep a distance between the unicorns and anyone else.

She was less afraid now—and she was grateful to Joseph for that.

From a long way off Moonsilver would look like a noble's horse.

So would Avamir.

No one would be able to tell that she wasn't a page—not unless they came close enough to see her Gypsy clothes.

When evening finally came, Heart left the steep road, her legs aching. She found another sheltered clearing, farther from the road. There were plum thickets to keep them hidden.

She took Moonsilver's armor off.

He galloped in circles, then rolled to scratch his back.

Heart made a tiny cook fire. She ate bread and apples and a broth made from herbed barley.

Kip sat quietly until she spread her blanket to lie down. Then he curled up close to her.

Heart's legs hurt. She wished for some of Ruth Oakes's meadowsweet salve.

Heart yawned.

She was tired.

But she forced herself to pull out her book and the half candle.

She hadn't practiced even once since they left Joseph's forge.

She had promised Tibbs she would.

And what the rude woman had forced her to read made her wonder. It had sounded as though there was a Royal House of Avamir somewhere—that it was *real*.

But where was it?

Heart opened the book carefully, looking for the page with the design of the rearing unicorns.

She stared at the perfect drawing.

The woman in Yolen's Crossing had read aloud to her. Her books had said the lords had hunted the unicorns in the forests.

Had they killed all but two of them?

Heart glanced up at Moonsilver and Avamir.

Were they the only unicorns left?

Heart looked at the words below the design.

She sounded out the words silently, then read

them aloud. "The Mountains of the Moon," it said beneath the drawing.

Heart took a deep breath and focused on the next line. "'The an . . . an . . . ,'" she began. Then she frowned.

It was a strange, long word.

It was the one Zim hadn't been able to read.

The word that followed it was odd too. Heart couldn't sound either one of them out.

She turned the page.

"'And so the off . . . offer was hon . . . hon . . . ,'" she read aloud, then stopped again.

Heart tightened her hands on the book.

Why couldn't she just *read* it?

Heart tried turning more pages. There were so many words. They seemed endless. And so many of them were long and complicated.

This book was much harder to read than the one the rude woman had carried.

Heart's candle flickered.

A little breeze was stirring.

She rested the book on her chest and looked up at the sky.

There was no moon.

The stars glittered.

Kip stretched, then snuggled close.

Heart pulled her blanket higher.

The breeze blew out her candle.

Heart thought about lighting it again. She knew she should practice reading. Then she closed her eyes.

She was so *tired*.

Her dreams rushed forward.

She dreamed she was running up a canyon. It was dark until the moon rose, wide and steady, filling the sky overhead.

Its light turned the mountains silver gray.

✦CHAPTER FIVE

"How much longer?"

"Just hurry and stop complaining!"

The shouts jolted Heart awake. She sat up straight, startled out of a deep sleep.

Kip scrambled to his feet.

The men's voices were coming from the road, beyond the plum thickets.

Heart was afraid. What if they stopped to argue? Would they see the unicorns through the leaves?

Kip growled. Heart took his muzzle in her hand. "No, Kip. Don't bark."

Avamir was wide awake, her head lifted, her nostrils flared.

Moonsilver sprang upright. His horn shone in

the early sun. Avamir stood more slowly, her eyes rimmed in white.

Heart picked up the book and her candle and shoved them into her carry-sack.

She kept glancing at the trees, her pulse quick.

The unicorns' white coats were as bright as spring snow.

If the men looked back and caught a glimpse of them through the branches . . .

Kip bared his teeth without making a sound.

"Stay out of the cakes," the first voice said angrily. "Can't you walk a little faster?"

"You be still," the second voice scolded. "It'll go on for a week. How often is a new lord crowned?"

"Once in a lifetime," the first voice admitted. They were passing, and their voices were fading. "But it isn't a real lord, anyway," the man was saying. "The uncle will . . ."

The voice went on, getting too far away to hear. After a moment the whispery sighs of the forest were the only sounds. Then Heart heard another voice—a woman's this time.

Heart rushed to buckle on Moonsilver's armor.

Her hands were trembling.

When the unicorns were ready, she stopped at the edge of the road and looked left and right.

Heart could see people in *both* directions.

She stepped forward, her pulse speeding up again.

The best thing to do was to stay between the other travelers.

At first it was easy.

It got harder.

Every little lane that joined the High Road had a few people on it.

There were more little roads all the time.

Like creeks joining a river, each town road carried a current of people and wagons.

By midmorning the High Road was full, a tangle of carts and crowds.

The unicorns pretended that Heart was leading them along.

People stared at Moonsilver for a moment, then went back to talking.

These people were farmers and villagers, Heart realized. They were interested in the fancy armor. But they didn't know or care how Heart should be dressed.

Heart made sure the unicorns walked at the pace of the crowds around them.

She was careful not to meet anyone's eyes.

The countryside was rocky and steep as the road continued upward. Then, finally, at midday it began to descend, going downhill at last.

They passed more towns.

By afternoon Heart and the unicorns were squeezed between a wagon full of caged pheasants and six chatting women.

The women carried bulging bags over their shoulders. Heart knew what was in them. She could smell fresh-baked bread.

Kip could too.

He dropped back.

He walked beside one of the women, looking up at her.

She bent down to pat his head. He gave her a

wet doggy kiss on the cheek.

The woman laughed aloud.

Heart kept glancing over her shoulder.

She couldn't let go of the unicorns' halters. People had to think they were horses—that they needed to be led along or they might stray.

Kip was bowing now, Heart saw. He was using his Gypsy-show tricks to charm the women.

"Look at that!" the woman said, getting her friends to watch Kip too.

"Kip!" Heart called. "Come!" She met the woman's eyes. "I'm sorry he's bothering you," she said politely.

The woman smiled widely at her. "No bother at all!"

"Kip!" Heart called again.

This time he came, his ears and tail lowered.

He walked beside Moonsilver, sulking.

"Don't be so friendly," Heart scolded him in a low voice. "What will I do if they start asking questions?"

"Beautiful horses, dearie," the woman called

out to her. "And such a lovely little dog."

Heart nodded without turning.

"Is your master in Bidenfast for the festival?"

Heart glared at Kip. He whined and lowered his head as though he understood why she was angry.

"That's where we are going," Heart said carefully. "I have friends there."

The woman nodded pleasantly. "Well, if you like dog tricks, be sure to see the Gypsy show."

Heart turned. "Gypsy show?"

The woman nodded. "There might be a horse trained to act like a unicorn, people are saying. And they have wirewalkers and balancers and music—and two or three trained dogs."

"It sounds grand," Heart said as evenly as she could. "Are you sure they will be there?"

The woman nodded. "My cousin's wife's friend is a guardsman. He says the young lord's uncle wanted them there."

Heart turned away, glancing at Moonsilver and Avamir.

They looked like bored horses, their heads and

tails low, their eyes half closed as they walked.

"He's a bad one," the woman whispered. "The uncle. He takes shares off his villages' crops till the folk nearly starve."

"Hush yourself," one of the woman's friends warned. The woman's eyes widened, and Heart saw her glance toward Moonsilver.

"I mean, I heard that once," she said quickly. "I'm sure it wasn't true."

She dropped back to walk with her friends, her cheeks flushed.

Heart knew the woman thought she was a stable page—some low-ranking nobility—because of Moonsilver's armor. Heart wanted to explain that she was a villager too.

But she didn't dare.

The weary day went on. Heart's spirits sank as the hours passed.

It only got worse.

That night Moonsilver had to stand in his armor.

There were so many people close by that Heart didn't dare take it off.

She saw farmers glancing her way.

She knew they thought she was both cruel and lazy.

Why else would she make her lord's horse sleep so uncomfortably?

Heart felt terrible. The cart horses and wagon mules around them were better off than poor Moonsilver that night.

She lay awake, staring at the sky.

Thinking, she turned her silver bracelet around and around on her wrist. She would have to enter the city of Bidenfast.

It would be dangerous.

But she had no choice.

The Gypsies were probably fine, but what if they weren't? What if they needed her help? She had to find out.

✦CHAPTER SIX

The next morning the crowds were even thicker.

Road dust hung in the air.

Kip kept sneezing.

"There it is!" someone finally shouted.

Heart looked up.

The city of Bidenfast had been built high on a hill.

The houses reminded Heart of Derrytown. They were tall, and some of them were pretty.

But the castle towered above the town.

Its stone was the color of storm clouds.

Heart moved forward, trapped by the crowds.

She kept Kip close.

Avamir and Moonsilver walked side by side, placing their hooves carefully.

Slowly the river of people and wagons neared the city gates.

Heart saw guardsmen standing on both sides.

"Keep your head down," Heart murmured, hoping Moonsilver wouldn't start prancing to show off his armor.

Avamir nickered softly.

Moonsilver stopped, pulling his halter from Heart's hand.

She turned, startled, as he dropped back and lowered his head.

His long, armor-covered horn fit against his mother's side.

Heart watched carefully.

The guards kept scanning the crowds as they passed through.

None of them seemed to notice the unicorns.

Heart exhaled as they inched their way forward.

Heart looked up the hill, staring at the castle.

It reminded her of Dunraven's. Maybe all castles looked cold and hard.

Easing to one side of the throngs of people,

Heart finally managed to turn up a less crowded street.

"Do you know where the Gypsies are?" she asked a farmer leading a mule.

The man shook his head. "Just got here last night. I can't find a stable for Worthy." He patted his mule. "Can't even find my brothers. We were to meet at the gates, but . . ."

He trailed off, and Heart nodded. It would be impossible to find anyone in the crowds outside the city.

She wished the man good fortune and went on, walking up the street, then turning down a lane with tall houses. A boardwalk rose above the dust. Heart heard women laughing and looked up.

Two women dressed in city clothing were walking toward her.

She asked them the same question.

"In the square below the East Gate, aren't they, Mara?" one woman asked the other.

"The Gypsies?" the second woman answered.

"No. They're on the green above the old library building."

The first woman nodded. "That's right. The Gypsies are on the hill. It's the trained bears that are caged by East Gate."

"Library?" Heart asked. Joseph had used the word. "Are there books there?"

The woman frowned. "I don't know. No one goes there but the nobles."

"Can you tell me the way?" Heart asked.

The woman began talking and pointing.

Heart listened carefully.

The directions were easy.

The hard part was getting through the streets.

The whole city was a maze of wagons and carts.

Men sold cakes and breads from pushcarts.

Tents of bright cloth had been set up everywhere.

Women were selling embroidered blouses, baskets, silver earrings, cabbages, leather boots, and a hundred other things.

It was like a market square that filled the whole city.

Heart had to let go of Moonsilver's halter so they could walk single file.

She kept glancing back at him, then at Kip, as she wove a path through the crowds.

Heart was tired and hungry.

She could tell the unicorns were weary too.

She longed to be back in the forest, camping in a meadow where they could all rest.

But the noise of the crowds beat at her ears.

It blended with the colors and smells until she felt nearly dizzy.

When they finally made the last turn, Heart looked up the wide street.

There was a huge stone building on one side. Lions carved out of marble were at the gates.

Beyond it Heart saw trees and more houses. Then the street narrowed and went up a hill.

At the very end of the lane trees framed a little meadow. Heart saw a blue wagon.

It was Binney's!

Joy and relief lifting her feet, Heart walked faster.

Kip barked and raced in a circle.

Heart called to him to stay close.

Avamir raised her head and nickered.

Moonsilver began to prance, and the plumes on his armor swayed and nodded.

When they got to the steepest part of the hill, Heart could see more of the wagons. There was Zim's and Talia's aunt's and the red one that belonged to Davey and his parents.

Heart's eyes were stinging, and she hoped that she wouldn't start crying when she saw Binney.

Avamir shook her mane.

Heart reached out to touch the mare's neck.

Binney was going to be so surprised. They all would be.

There would be food and laughter.

And Heart knew she'd get to sleep in a soft bed inside Binney's wagon tonight and . . .

"Page!"

Heart glanced to one side, not understanding at first.

"Page! Come here!" the guard shouted a second time.

Heart realized the guard was talking to her, and she stumbled to a halt. Avamir and Moonsilver stopped with her. Kip whined and circled them.

"Yes, sir?" Heart said politely.

"Stay away from the Gypsies."

Heart stared at him. "Why?"

The guard laughed harshly. "Because our new young lord has ordered it. People were thronging up here to get a look."

"But I know them and—," Heart began.

The guard laughed again, cutting her off. He shook his head in disbelief, then pointed back down the hill. "The stable on Coal Dust Road is for the lords' horses." He stepped squarely in front of Heart, scowling.

Heart fought tears. The Gypsies were camped on the other side of the line of wagons.

No one could see her.

No one would know she was here.

The guard took a step toward her. "Did you hear me? Who is your master?"

Heart let out a breath and lowered her eyes. "Yes, sir. I heard you. Thank you, sir."

She walked in a wide half circle, pretending to lead the unicorns as though they were horses.

Kip trotted close to Avamir's side, his head tilted in confusion.

He whimpered.

Heart walked back down the hill, her eyes full of tears.

+CHAPTER SEVEN

Heart had no intention of going to the royal stables.

She could not imagine a more dangerous place for the unicorns.

She walked in circles for a long time.

She traded a few songs on her flute for enough pennies to buy bread for herself and Kip.

She bought carrots for the unicorns and some cracked corn.

Then, as the day passed, she wondered where she should go to camp.

The streets were clearing out. It was getting chilly.

Heart rounded a corner and saw a line of guardsmen walking toward her.

People moved ahead of them like herded cattle.

Heart stopped.

She turned around, hurrying back the way she had come.

She headed down another street, thinking hard.

Maybe she should leave the city and make her way back to the forest to camp. But it was so far, and they were all so tired.

"Curfew!" someone called.

Heart looked up, puzzled.

"No one allowed on the streets past six," a guard was shouting. "Make your way to your lodgings and camps now."

Heart saw another line of guards. People walked in front of them, too. Behind them the street was empty.

"Page!" one of them shouted. "The stables are that way!" He pointed. "I'll show you," he called when she didn't respond. He walked toward her, stern faced.

Terrified, Heart could only follow him through the streets.

He walked fast.

"There," he said after a few minutes. "Is your lord riding this one in the parades?" He jerked his thumb at Moonsilver.

Heart smiled, trying not to look as frightened as she was.

"Here's another one!" the man shouted to the guards outside the stables. Then he turned to leave.

A tall man walked Heart inside. "There are a few empty stalls. Just look until you find one."

Heart nodded, her hand trembling on the unicorns' halters. Kip trotted silently, his ears and tail down.

The stables were dim.

Heart walked up the aisles with fear-stiff knees.

All the pages stared. Their faces were closed, wary. They looked at her with disdain as she passed.

They all wore bright, new tunics. The boys had caps. The girls kept their hair short and neat.

"What happened to that mare?" one of the girls asked as they passed. It was not a kind question. Her voice was sharp and sneering.

Heart kept walking.

Whispers floated down the stable aisle, surrounding her.

"What country lord sent the likes of her here?"

"The armor is filthy."

"The mare is skinny. I'd be ashamed."

Heart looked at Avamir. It was true. They had traveled hard since they left the forge.

"The one next to mine is empty."

This voice was soft. Heart looked up. A girl was gesturing at her. "Down there. At the end of this row."

Heart nodded. "Thanks." She was afraid to say more. Her voice was unsteady.

If the unicorns were spotted, there would be no escape. There were guards everywhere.

She opened the stall door with shaking hands.

Moonsilver and Avamir stepped into it. Heart looked around. The hayrack was full. There was a big oaken bucket.

"Stay quiet," she whispered to Avamir. "Keep Moonsilver calm. I'll be right back with water."

Kip whined, and she looked down at him. "We

can't go see Binney yet," she told him. "We just can't."

"I do that too." The girl's voice startled Heart into stumbling backward. She kicked her carry-sack, and her book slid onto the straw bedding.

"Sorry!" the girl said. "I only meant to say I talk to my mare too."

Heart nodded and pushed the book out of sight with her toe.

The girl climbed the gate planks. She leaned forward. "My name is Anna."

Heart introduced herself.

"What a beautiful name," Anna said as they clasped hands.

Heart set her carry-sack at the back of the stall. Then she picked up the bucket.

Anna showed her the well.

Heart lowered the bucket, then raised it, dripping and full.

"What lord do you serve?" Anna asked on the way back. "Will you be allowed to go to the Gypsy shows?"

Heart caught her breath. She didn't answer.

"I can't," Anna said. "Lord Dunraven never lets us out of the stables."

Anna followed Heart back to the stall. Heart set the bucket in the corner, glancing nervously over her shoulder.

Kip drank first.

A sudden murmur of pages' voices rose in the stable, and Heart turned to look.

Through the wide doors, outlined against the evening sky, Heart saw a boy.

He was sitting down. It looked like he was floating along at shoulder height.

Heart stared.

"That's him in the chair," Anna whispered. "The new lord. He's sick all the time, people say."

"Why is he here?" Heart whispered.

"I don't know," Anna answered. Then she took a quick breath. "Lord Dunraven!"

Anna disappeared into her stall. Heart heard the sound of a stable rake a second later.

Heart's breathing quickened.

It *was* Lord Dunraven, walking beside the odd, high chair.

There were five or six other men too.

Heart narrowed her eyes. Four of them were carrying the chair. Long poles rested on their shoulders.

Lord Dunraven walked to one side, talking with another man.

Their tunics looked like silk.

Heart could see the flash of silver buttons.

The men carrying the chair wore rougher cloth.

The hurried sounds of currycombing, raking, and leather polishing spread through the huge barn as the pages noticed the lords coming.

Heart slipped back into her stall.

She tried to think.

It would look odd to have Moonsilver in his armor inside the stable—but she could hardly take it off now.

She glanced over the stall planks.

Young Lord Irmaedith looked weary and ill.

Heart glanced at Kip. "Be quiet. Not a sound."

Then she looked at Avamir. The mare was standing tall, her head lifted to watch.

"It's the new lord," Heart whispered. "He's just a sickly boy."

The strange chair moved steadily up the stable aisle.

Heart could hear the carriers murmuring.

As they got closer she understood; it was a rhyme, recited to time their steps.

Lord Dunraven's raspy voice cut through the noise. "How many horses does he want to see?"

No one answered him.

Avamir shook her mane. The tiny Gypsy bells jingled.

Heart's pulse hammered at her wrists and temples.

"Shhhh," she whispered to Avamir.

The mare shook her mane again.

Heart saw the boy's eyes open wider.

He sat up straighter, turning his head. He was looking for the source of the jingling.

The bracelet on Heart's wrist tightened.

Frantic, she leaned close to Avamir. "Be still."

Heart glanced back.

The boy had slumped in the chair again.

Heart let out a long breath. They would just walk past, she told herself.

They'd turn the corner and head back up the next aisle. It was a big stable. There were a hundred horses or more. The boy wouldn't notice the unicorns.

Then Avamir walked closer to the gate.

Heart pushed at her shoulder.

"Avamir!" Heart pleaded in a whisper.

Dunraven's deep, rasping voice was getting louder. He was talking about the cold nights, complaining about the small hearth fires in the castle.

Avamir pushed her head out over the stall door.

She shook her mane again.

The bells tinkled.

"Stop there," the boy lord said in a high, quivery voice. "That white mare."

Heart gripped the rake, leaning on it, her pulse thundering in her ears.

✦CHAPTER EIGHT

The boy bent forward in his chair and reached out to touch Avamir's forehead. Heart saw him trace her scar, his hand gentle, his eyes sad.

On the other side of the carriers, Lord Dunraven continued talking. "There's still far too many," he was saying. "The fewer books the better."

Heart glanced at the boy lord. His skin was the color of eggshells. He was patting Avamir, staring at Moonsilver in delight.

"I've ordered more burnings," the man talking to Lord Dunraven said clearly.

Heart looked up.

The boy turned. "Burnings?"

Lord Dunraven cleared his throat. "Books. It's time to get rid of the old legends once and for all."

The boy looked troubled. "My father loved books," he said politely. "So do I."

"You'd like them less if you could ride and hunt," the man next to Lord Dunraven said.

"That isn't true," the boy said.

The man frowned. "Your father was a fool to coddle you."

Heart saw the boy's eyes flood with tears. "Uncle Stevenar, please don't insult him now."

The man laughed gently. "I know you're sad that he died. I am too. But he was weak. I intend to be strong."

"I am the new lord," the boy said quietly. "Not you, Uncle."

The man laughed again, less gently. "Worry tires you. I will handle all these things."

Heart saw the anger in the boy's eyes. But he slumped back in his chair and took a slow breath.

"Are you finished patting horses?" Lord Dunraven asked. He walked around the front of the chair.

Heart heard Anna gasp in the next stall, but Lord

Dunraven hadn't noticed her at all. He spit and glanced back at his companion. "Have you seen this style? It makes the horse look like a unicorn."

Heart froze, terrified.

The boy's uncle nodded. "It's used here, too."

Lord Dunraven shook his head in disgust, then turned away. "The young lord should rest before the crowning."

"I *am* very tired," the boy said softly.

Heart felt so sorry for him.

He looked miserable.

And his uncle was unkind and a bully.

Heart knew what she should do. It was dangerous. But it would be wrong *not* to do it.

"Moonsilver!" Heart whispered. "Touch him."

Avamir flicked her ears and turned to look at Heart.

"Tell Moonsilver to touch him," Heart breathed.

The boy looked dazed and ill. His eyes were half closed.

"We wish to leave now," Lord Dunraven said. The carriers stood straighter.

Avamir whickered softly.

Moonsilver lifted his head high.

One of the chair carriers began to count.

"One, two, three . . ."

They stepped forward on the count of four.

In that instant, Moonsilver reached out, his neck arched, lowering his horn.

Carefully, lightly as a moth wing, he touched the boy lord's lips.

Then he stepped backward, hanging his head as the chair moved off. Dunraven was talking again, walking close to the boy lord's uncle as they passed.

Heart saw the boy turn sharply and look back at her.

His eyes were wide.

His cheeks were flushed with pink.

Their eyes met for an instant.

Then the chair turned the corner and started up the next aisle.

✦CHAPTER NINE

Within ten minutes the barn was noisy again.

The pages relaxed and began talking, settling in for the night.

Heart was very glad the boy would be well now.

It had been the right thing to do.

But it had been foolish, too, and dangerous.

Would he realize what had happened?

If he did, would he tell his uncle and Lord Dunraven?

Heart paced back and forth while the other pages raked up piles of clean straw for their beds and washed their faces in the water buckets.

It would be impossible to leave before morning.

Without the crowds to hide in, the guards would stop her the instant she left the barn.

Slowly, one by one, the voices in the stalls quieted.

The horses lay down, and Heart could hear them sleeping, a steady lullaby of hay-sweet breath.

Mice began to rustle in the grain boxes.

Then, after a long time, even they quieted and went to sleep.

Heart sat in a corner of the stall, waiting for morning. She was far too worried to sleep.

But after most of the night was gone, as the moon was rising, she began to wonder if things would be all right.

Wouldn't the boy have told someone by now if he was going to tell?

It was possible he had no idea what had happened.

He certainly had a healer trying to help him.

Probably he'd been given herbs.

Maybe the royal healers would think the herbs had finally cured him.

Heart sighed. She was so weary.

She lay down.

She closed her eyes and waited for her dreams to come.

"Pssst!"

Heart was instantly awake. "Anna? Is that you?"

"No," came the whispered answer.

There was a shuffling sound as someone climbed over the gate and jumped lightly into the straw bedding.

Kip growled.

Avamir switched her tail.

Moonsilver was standing, dozing. He lifted his head calmly.

The visitor lit a candle. In the amber light Heart saw a merry-eyed boy whose once pale cheeks were now rosy.

"They made me go get crowned," he said. "But after that I looked in my books. I know what happened."

"Did something happen?" Heart asked carefully.

"I heard you talk to the mare," the boy said. "Then she whinnied and then the stallion . . . touched me." The boy bowed toward Avamir and

Moonsilver. "I came to thank you all."

Heart was silent.

The boy looked at his own hand. He clenched his fist. "I feel strong! I've never felt strong."

He looked over the candle flame at Heart. "Unicorns!" He breathed the word. "No one thinks they are real."

Heart leaned toward him. "Don't tell anyone," she pleaded. "All the lords will chase us. They will all want to . . ." She stopped, blushing, remembering who she was talking to.

"How may I repay you?" the new Lord Irmaedith asked.

"Are the Gypsies safe?" Heart whispered. "They had a fake unicorn once. It was part of the show. Lord Dunraven knew about it, and I—"

"I will protect them," the boy lord interrupted. "May they do the rest of their shows?"

Heart nodded. "If they can leave safely afterward."

He smiled and promised again, lifting the candle. "You think of your friends before yourself?"

Heart was silent.

The boy grinned at her, a flash of white teeth in the candlelight. "You are a true heart. Ask another favor."

Heart looked into his eyes. "Promise they will be safe?"

He nodded. "You have my word."

Heart took a deep breath. "Do you know anything about the Royal House of Avamir?"

The boy sighed. "If you could read—"

"I am learning," Heart told him.

He grinned again. "Then there is a book I will give you gladly. Is there nothing else you want?"

"I need to leave Bidenfast," Heart told him. "It's too dangerous here for the . . . horses."

The young lord nodded. "I'll go get the book and a few guards. I'll say you must leave early. They can escort you back to the High Road. Or farther?" he asked, looking up at her.

Heart shook her head. "No. I can camp somewhere and wait for the Gypsies."

"Maybe one day we can be friends," he said. "I have none."

Heart started to answer.

He was already turning, blowing out the candle.

He climbed the gate.

She heard his light footfalls as he left.

✦CHAPTER TEN

Heart hid the young lord's gift book deep in her carry-sack. He took her hand in farewell and flashed her another grin. "I am Lord Irmaedith now," he whispered, "but my name is Seth." He bowed. "Good-bye, Heart. Travel safely."

Then he sprang back over the gate, and she heard him murmur to the guards.

"Good-bye," Heart whispered.

It was strange leaving the stables with the guards. Heart knew the other pages would think she had broken some law.

The guards rode in silence behind her as she walked the unicorns back out the gates, down the long hill, and onto the High Road.

Then they reined in.

One of them gave her a bag of food. There were even carrots for the unicorns.

The guards waited as she started off.

After a moment she heard them ride away.

What was left of that long night passed easily, quietly.

By morning Heart was too tired to go any farther. She found a good clearing with an icy creek and made camp. It was above the road, with a stand of sycamores to keep people from seeing the unicorns.

There were only a few wagons coming past Bidenfast.

When Heart heard wheels creaking, she would look, then go back to her reading.

Lord Irmaedith's book was a little hard for her.

But she was determined to read it, no matter how long it took.

The book was worn, the cover dented and rubbed.

It had childish pencil drawings on some of the pages.

It was a storybook. Lord Irmaedith had told her that many royal children were given story-books to read.

Heart loved the stories.

One was about a unicorn healing a sick girl.

Another was a sad tale of unicorns being hunted.

A third talked about a place where the unicorns had hidden from the hunters.

Heart was sure the stories weren't just stories.

They were *history*—things that had really happened.

A fourth story told her that the Royal House of Avamir was in Lord Levin's lands, close to Lord Kaybale's border.

The morning that she heard creaking wheels mixed with the jingle of Gypsy bells, Heart stood up and brushed off her skirt.

Kip barked.

Avamir and Moonsilver cantered toward the road.

Moonsilver was lifting his hooves high.

Heart smiled. The Gypsies had never seen his beautiful armor. He was showing off.

Heart laughed aloud at Binney's joyous shout.

Then she ran toward her friends.

THE UNICORN'S SECRET

Experience the Magic

When the battered mare Heart Trilby takes in presents her with a silvery white foal, Heart's life is transformed into one of danger, wonder, and miracles beyond her wildest imaginings. Read about Heart's thrilling quest in

THE UNICORN'S SECRET # (1):
Moonsilver
0-689-84269-4

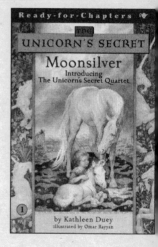

THE UNICORN'S SECRET # (2):
The Silver Thread
0-689-84270-8

THE UNICORN'S SECRET # (3):
The Silver Bracelet
0-689-84271-6

THE UNICORN'S SECRET # (4):
The Mountains of the Moon
0-689-84272-4

THE UNICORN'S SECRET # (5):
The Sunset Gates
0-689-85347-5

ALADDIN PAPERBACKS
Simon & Schuster Children's Publishing Division • www.SimonSaysKids.com

Read